IMAGINE THAT™

Licensed exclusively to Imagine That Publishing Ltd
Tide Mill Way, Woodbridge, Suffolk, IP12 1AP, UK
www.imaginethat.com
Copyright © 2021 Imagine That Group Ltd
All rights reserved
4 6 8 9 7 5 3
Manufactured in China

Written by Kitty Taylor
Illustrated by Aleksandra Szmidt

ISBN 978-1-80105-168-2

A catalogue record for this book is available from the British Library

All My Goodnight Hugs

A ready-for-bed story

Written by
Kitty
Taylor

Illustrated by
Aleksandra
Szmidt

It's time for bed so ...

I hug Daddy.

I hug my little sister.

I hug my
big brother.

I hug Grandma.

I hug Grandpa.

I hug my new bear.

I hug my
narwhal.

I hug my dinosaur.

I hug my
unicorn.

I hug my monkey.

I hug my dragon.

I hug my pink bunny
and my white bunny, too.

I hug my whale.

I hug my
cat.

I hug my raccoon.

I hug my panda.

I hug my
elephant.

Then I climb into
my full bed ...

... and I hug
Mummy.

I hug my favourite
bear as I snuggle down.

Goodnight everyone.
Sleep tight.

Goodnight
hugs are
the best!